Malaika's Costume

Nadia L. Hohn

PICTURES BY

Irene Luxbacher

GROUNDWOOD BOOKS

HOUSE OF ANANSI PRESS

TORONTO BERKELEY

Text copyright © 2016 by Nadia L. Hohn
Illustrations copyright © 2016 by Irene Luxbacher
Published in Canada and the USA in 2016 by Groundwood Books

Groundwood Books / House of Anansi Press
110 Spadina Avenue, Suite 801, Toronto, Ontario M5V 2K4
or c/o Publishers Group West
1700 Fourth Street, Berkeley, CA 94710

We acknowledge for their financial support of our publishing program the Canada Council for the Arts, the Ontario Arts Council and the Government of Canada.

Canada Council
for the Arts

Conseil des Arts
du Canada

ONTARIO ARTS COUNCIL
CONSEIL DES ARTS DE L'ONTARIO
an Ontario government agency
un organisme du gouvernement de l'Ontario

With the participation of the Government of Canada
Avec la participation du gouvernement du Canada   Canadä

Library and Archives Canada Cataloguing in Publication
Hohn, Nadia L., author
Malaika's costume / written by Nadia L. Hohn ; and illustrated by Irene Luxbacher.
Issued in print and electronic formats.
ISBN 978-1-55498-754-2 (bound). — ISBN 978-1-55498-755-9 (pdf)
I. Luxbacher, Irene, illustrator II. Title.
PS8615.O396M35 2016   jC813'.6   C2015-904632-7
C2015-904633-5

The illustrations were done in mixed media, graphite and oils on paper.
Design by Michael Solomon
Printed and bound in Malaysia

For my dear students at Africentric Alternative School. To every child with big dreams, one day they can come true. — NH

For my family, with love — IL

cassava: The starchy root of a tropical shrub, which can be used for food.

Jab Molassie: A carnival mas (masquerade) character who is an acrobatic devil, from the French "Diable Mélasse," or Molasses Devil.

kaiso: Music that originated in West Africa and was sung by enslaved people in the Caribbean, containing a story with a hidden meaning. It evolved into calypso music.

Moko Jumbie: A stilt walker of West African origin whose height was traditionally associated with the ability to see evil.

Obeah: Practices of West African origin found in the Caribbean that incorporate magic, mysticism and sorcery in combination with Christian beliefs.

pan: A musical instrument made from an oil drum, also called a steel drum or steelpan, originating in Trinidad.

Pierrot: A carnival mas (masquerade) character who carries a pistol or whip and is known for long speeches and verbal dueling.

Rastaman: A man who practices Rastafari, a way of life that began in Jamaica but has African, Jewish and Christian roots.

Soca: Music that developed in the 1970s in Trinidad and Tobago, when calypso music was influenced by Indo-Caribbean rhythms, R&B, soul and disco.

I CLOSE MY EYES and dance. I am a beautiful peacock. Each feather shimmers — green, gold, turquoise and brown.

Grandma say, "Girl, I think you is definitely my granddaughter for true."

This is the first carnival time with Mummy gone.
"She in Canada," Uncle Ewart say. "Canada's
a place where she can get a good job. She going
to make a better life for you and Granny."

This is the first carnival time with Mummy gone. "She in Canada," Uncle Ewart say. "Canada's a place where she can get a good job. She going to make a better life for you and Granny."

I CLOSE MY EYES and dance. I am a beautiful peacock. Each feather shimmers — green, gold, turquoise and brown.

Grandma say, "Girl, I think you is definitely my granddaughter for true."

Canada is cold like an icebox and something they call snow is on the ground, Mummy tell me. She send me pictures, too. The snow look like coconut sky juice. She say that children play in it and build man with it.

What a sticky mess!

If there's so many jobs in Canada, how come Grandma
and I have been waiting so long, long for the money
Mummy say she would send to make my costume?

Carnival soon come, and everyone getting their costume ready.

Michael and Junior are playing Jab Molassie in the Kiddie Carnival. They wearing briefs and blue paint. Ravina and Shelly are red hibiscus. They wearing their saris and looking like brides.

Malcolm and Marcus are stilt-dancing
Moko Jumbies. They look like giraffes.
Even the Johnson baby, Ivan, has a Pierrot
costume. He's still
crawling!
Everyone practice
their dance moves.
Everyone except
me. I don't feel like
dancing anymore.

Today a letter come, but after Grandma open it, she look sad. I just know what the writing say, and big teardrops roll down my face.

Grandma go to her room. She come back with an old red cardboard suitcase that I never see before. She pull out a green and purple costume covered in gold sequins and dangling ribbon.

"This was my carnival costume when I was a girl."

Grandma make me put on the tired costume. It smell
funny and it dusty. The costume squeeze my belly and
some of the sequins fall off. I feel hot and itchy.

"Grandma, I don't like it. I won't wear this tear-up old thing," I say, and with that I pull off the costume, hearing it rip. I run, run, run with my hot, dry feet.

I pass two goats drinking from a puddle. I pass a few neighbors' yards — Mr. Da Silva, Ms. Blake, Pastor Simms — and I pass the clap-hand church where Grandma sometime take me. I see the old men in front of the little shop. Across the street, I see Menelik the Rastaman, who sell us the cassava chips and jelly coconut that I like so much. I almost reach the Obeah lady's old house at the end of the street.

I stop. I don't know where else to go.

Then I begin to hear a song that I know. It's playing on someone's stereo. It goes, "I started to beat pan at the age of six … Me grandmother tell me … It is true we are poor but we have dignity …"

This is one of Grandma's favorite kaiso songs.

I run to Ms. Chin the tailor lady around the corner.

"Do you have any throwaway cloth? I just need a few rags," I say.

"Chile, is Granny making you some more dolls?" she ask in her singsong kind of voice.

I think about my two pretty rag dolls, CeeCee and DeeDee, sitting on my bed.

"No, ma'am. For a surprise," I say.

Ms. Chin turn around and go into a room. She come back with a big red plastic bag. It flowing over with pieces of ripped-up cloth, all in different colors. I smile.

"Thank you, ma'am," I say, and then I run all the way back home.

I bang the door open.

"Grandma, Grandma, guess what I find?" I yell, while holding the handle of the bag tight.

"Shhhhh. Hush, chile," Grandma say. She look at me with a sad face, then I start to cry.

"I'm sorry. I didn't mean to run off and say those things."

"All right, Malaika, you do better now." She smile. "Now, what you bring?"

I show her the bag of cloth, and I smile when I tell her my idea.

Then it's Grandma's turn to surprise me. While I ran away, she fix the costume and wipe it clean with soap and rosewater. Then she sprinkle a little baby powder inside so it smell sweet and fresh. I see the clean costume hanging on the clothing line, drying in the sun.

"It smell nice, Grandma," I say.

"Well, my dear," she say, "what will you be this year?"

"A rainbow peacock like the one in my dream."

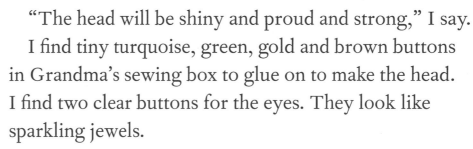

"The head will be shiny and proud and strong," I say.

I find tiny turquoise, green, gold and brown buttons in Grandma's sewing box to glue on to make the head. I find two clear buttons for the eyes. They look like sparkling jewels.

"The body, round and full of bright feathers, Grandma."

We rip, rip, rip small pieces of the colorful cloth, then tie them on to the body of the costume.

"Oooh, red chiffon, blue silk, jade lace, purple ribbon," Grandma whisper.

The words sound like music to my ears.

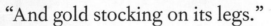

"And gold stocking on its legs."

Grandma pull out some crinkled stocking from the suitcase and a pair of slippers. There are some holes in the stocking, but Grandma help me to patch them up with pieces of cloth.

"Grandma, this rainbow peacock have patchwork legs," I laugh.

We glue, sew and tie the cloth onto the body. Grandma even help me make cuffs for my arms out of copper cloth so that it look like wings. I twist in some gold wires to add extra feathers.

I carefully pull the peacock bodysuit on. Then Grandma put on my peacock head, just so. I look in the mirror. The costume fit me, and I shine from head to toe.

"Who looking so lovely? Girl, this costume look better than ever," Grandma say, and she is right. I am even more beautiful than the peacock in my dreams.

The next morning, I jump out of bed.
"It's time, Grandma! It's time!"
I put on the costume again, real slow, but then I start
to feel bad. It was Mummy who used to help dress me for
carnival.

"Grandma, can we take some pictures today? I want
to show Mummy."

"Of course, chile. Your mother wouldn't want
to miss this and she would be so proud you make
your costume," she say.

Grandma take me to the streets of the Kiddie Carnival parade, where all the people are bouncing and dancing to the music. Soca and calypso rhythms fill the street.

I see Ms. Chin.

"Wow! Look what you've made. You look beautiful, darling," she say.

"Who's that coming down the road? Carnival queen?" Uncle Ewart laughs.

I march out to the front like a proud peacock. I turn around and I dance, dance, dance.